Collect the special coins in this book.
You will earn one gold coin for
every chapter you read.

Once you have finished all the chapters,
find out what to do with your gold coins at
the back of the book.

With special thanks to Conrad Mason

For Ida Mason

www.beastquest.co.uk

ORCHARD BOOKS

First published in Great Britain in 2020 by The Watts Publishing Group

1 3 5 7 9 10 8 6 4 2

Text © 2020 Beast Quest Limited
Cover and inside illustrations by Steve Sims
© Beast Quest Limited 2020

Beast Quest is a registered trademark of Beast Quest Limited
Series created by Beast Quest Limited, London

A CIP catalogue record for this book is available from the British Library.

ISBN 978 1 40835 783 5

Printed in Great Britain

The paper and board used in this book are made from wood from responsible sources

Orchard Books
An imprint of Hachette Children's Group
Part of The Watts Publishing Group Limited
Carmelite House, 50 Victoria Embankment, London EC4Y 0DZ

An Hachette UK Company
www.hachette.co.uk
www.hachettechildrens.co.uk

PETORIX
THE WINGED SLICER

BY ADAM BLADE

ORCHARD

CONTENTS

STORY ONE

BEHOLD THE BEAST!

Petorix, the Winged Slicer... Her scales glittered as she flew. Vicious were her talons, and her foul tongue dripped with deadly venom. She ravaged the village, tore Errin's Hall apart.

Yet bold Tanner feared nothing. Astride Firepos the Flame Bird, he came to face the savage Beast. He soared up high, then down he leapt. His sword flashed like lightning. He grasped Petorix by her leathery wing and clung on as she fought to shake him.

But the warrior was too strong.

With a single blow, he struck her head from her shoulders. Then down they fell until she met her doom, perishing at last in the village she had wasted.

Thus Tanner, Master of the Beasts, vanquished the wicked Petorix!

Extract from *The Chronicles of Avantia*

THE SHADOW BEAST

"Here he comes!" cried Elenna, clutching Tom's arm. "The mightiest warrior in Avantia!"

Tom frowned. "I hope I never have to face him in battle!"

They looked at each other, and both burst out laughing.

Tom and Elenna were sitting on a pair of hay bales in the courtyard of

King Hugo's palace. It was a sunny afternoon, and Captain Harkman was playing with Prince Thomas. The one-year-old baby gurgled happily as the captain hoisted him up into the saddle of an old donkey.

"Easy does it, Your Highness," grunted Harkman. He held the squirming infant firmly.

"Tommy may not be ready to guard the palace *quite* yet," said Elenna.

"Laugh while you can," said Daltec, sternly. The young magician was holding on to the donkey's reins. "Young Thomas may be Master of the Beasts one day."

"I certainly hope so," chuckled Tom. "I could do with a rest!" He darted over to take the reins from Daltec.

"All Tommy needs is a Beast to fight," said Elenna.

Daltec nodded. "Allow me…" He stepped back, lifting his hands. His fingers twitched, and a ball of green light took shape between them. Then with a sudden flash, it transformed into a tiny green dragon, no bigger than a cat. The dragon flew up above the donkey, and Prince Thomas flapped at it with his pudgy hands.

Elenna stood and bowed low. "Hail, Master of the Beasts!" she said, and everyone chuckled.

Just then, a shout came from the battlements above. "Captain Harkman, sir!" A guard was pointing his spear at something beyond the walls.

Daltec flicked his hands, and the

dragon disappeared in a puff of green smoke.

"I'll handle this," said Tom, passing the reins to Elenna. He grinned at Harkman, who was still holding Prince Thomas. "You've got your hands full!"

Tom took up his sword and shield from beside the hay bale, then raced up the steps to the top of the wall. Shielding his eyes against the sun, he spotted something speeding across a field towards the City – a cart, pulled by a large black horse with a blanket across its back. The cart bumped and jolted, and its driver bounced up and down with it. She was an old woman, with a shawl wrapped around her head and shoulders.

Her voice carried towards them
on the wind. It was faint at first, but
getting louder. "Let me in, please! A
Beast is chasing me!"

Tom peered hard at the horizon,
where something had just swooped out
from behind a cloud. *Far too big to be a*

bird. "Open the gates!" he roared.

The chains of the drawbridge rattled, and the wood groaned as the bridge fell across the moat. The old woman flicked her reins and drove the rumbling cart across. At once the guards began to haul the drawbridge shut again.

The Beast came soaring towards them on a pair of dark wings, a long tail like a serpent's coiling behind it.

All along the wall, guards took up the cry: "We're under attack!"

Tom turned to see Captain Harkman running to the top of the steps. Below, Daltec was holding Prince Thomas, and Elenna was picking up her bow and quiver from where she'd left them on the ground.

"Archers!" roared Harkman. "Form a line!"

Bowmen spilled from the turrets at either end of the wall, clattering into position. Their bowstrings creaked as they fitted arrows and drew back, ready to fire.

"On my command!" called Harkman from the top of the wall.

"Wait!" Tom held up a hand, and the captain turned in surprise. "It might be a Good Beast," Tom explained. "I can find out what it wants."

He drew on the power of the ruby of Torgor, and felt the warmth of the magic flowing into him. He spoke with his mind. *Why have you come here?*

But if the Beast heard him, it made

no reply. And it was almost upon them, blotting out the sun. Its massive jaws gaped wide…

Whsssshhh! One of the archers had let fly. The arrow arced through the air and sliced into the body of the Beast. But it sailed on through, meeting no resistance.

Tom was just reaching for his sword hilt, when the Beast's shadowy body rippled… then collapsed a black smoke that drifted up into the sky. Tom blinked. Almost at once, the smoke had vanished. The sun shone again, as though nothing had happened.

Gasps and murmurs ran among the guards and archers on the walls.

"What in the name of King

Hugo…?" said Captain Harkman.

"A cheap magic trick," said Daltec. Tom saw that the wizard had joined them on the walls, still cradling the prince. Elenna was at his side. "It was just an illusion," Daltec explained. "Convincing, I must admit."

Tom frowned. *Why would anyone play such a trick?*

"Hang on," said Elenna. "Where did she go?"

She was staring down into the courtyard, and Tom suddenly remembered the old woman who had ridden into the palace. There was her cart, left abandoned by the wall, with the big black horse waiting patiently. But the old woman herself was nowhere to be seen.

"I don't like this," growled Captain Harkman.

BOOM! A deafening roar sounded from below, and the wall shuddered. Tom lost his footing and clutched the battlements, his ears ringing.

An explosion...and it sounded like it came from the treasury! He raced to the courtyard, heading for the great door that led to the palace vaults.

He was almost there when the door swung open with a hefty *thump.* A guard staggered out, bent over and coughing in a cloud of bitter smoke.

Tom barrelled past, through the doorway and down the dark steps. At the bottom, the metal door hung from its hinges, bent and blackened by fire. He ran on into the treasury, and skidded to a halt.

Everything looked normal – treasure chests, suits of armour and weapons piled up all around. But slumped against one wall was a man wearing nothing but boots and rough cotton underclothes. He looked up groggily, and Tom recognised him. *He's one of Harkman's best soldiers!*

Elenna and Harkman rushed in too.

"What's happening?" asked Elenna.

"Where's your uniform?" Harkman demanded.

The guard looked dazed. "Uniform? What uniform?"

Tom felt a lead weight settle in his stomach. *That guard I bumped into...the one who was coughing and covering their face...* Whoever it was,

they had stolen this man's uniform
to make their escape. It couldn't be a
coincidence that the old woman had
disappeared too.

"We've been tricked!" he exclaimed.

1

A CIRCLE OF STONE

Crouched behind a hay bale in the courtyard, Ria pulled off the helmet she had taken from the guard and shook her head to free her red mohawk. She chuckled to herself and checked that she still had the item she had stolen in the bag. *Yes*. It had been almost too easy.

Then a voice rose from the treasury. Tom's voice. "Intruder! Someone's in disguise as a guard!"

Ria's smile grew wider. *Time to go!*

Shouts went up from the guards all around, but Ria didn't care. *These idiots can't stop me.* She tore off the guard's cloak and drew the cat-o'-nine-tails from her belt. She flicked her wrist, and the strands crackled blue with electric charge.

Her steed was waiting, still harnessed to the cart. Ria whistled, and it reared up. The blanket slid from its back. Feathered wings unfurled from their hiding place.

One swift lash of the cat-o'-nine-tails, and the harness was severed. Ria vaulted on to the stallion's back and snatched up the reins.

"Stop her!" came a yell.

Ria dug her heels into the creature's flanks. With a lurch, the stallion left the ground.

As they swooped over the wall, wind rushing past, Ria caught a glimpse of the guards below, staring up with mouths open in astonishment. There was a *swish* as an arrow was shot from a bow, but it wasn't even close.

"Pathetic!" crowed Ria. She couldn't resist twitching the reins, guiding her stallion to circle above the palace. "Call yourselves soldiers, do you?"

Then her smile froze. There was Elenna, dashing out into the courtyard and fitting an arrow to her bowstring…

Before Ria could swoop away, the arrow whistled through the air.

Whhhsssshh!

Ria tugged hard at the reins, pulling the stallion's head back. It whinnied with shock, eyes rolling madly. The

arrow sailed past, just missing.

"Hopeless," croaked Ria, trying to hide how scared she had been. "Give my regards to Tom! I have a feeling I won't be seeing him again."

Even at a distance, Ria could make out Elenna's frown of confusion.

She cackled in triumph. *You'll see...* Then with a kick of her heels, the stallion soared off over the plains.

Ria glanced at the sun, using the reins to direct her steed towards the south-east. The ground rolled past below. Plains gave way to marshes. They flew over a little village, then gentle hills. When she glanced back, the City was already no more than a speck on the horizon. Ria's heart thumped with excitement. *So far, so good! My plan is working perfectly!*

The sky clouded over, and the air became chilly. Ria hunched down, staying close to the body of her stallion for warmth. Fog hung all around, and soon she could hardly see further than the wings beating on either side.

This must be it. The Misty Glen...

She twisted the reins. Down they flew, plunging through the fog. Sure enough, she began to make out grassy slopes leading down into a valley. And there, at the bottom, was a circle of bumpy, moss-covered stones. Nine of them, each one as big as an ogre. A low stone altar stood in the very centre of the circle.

Ria felt a thrill run through her. Her mother, Kensa, had told her of this place, and it had taken her a long time to find it.

The stallion's hooves bumped softly to the ground beside the circle. Ria slid from its back and left it to crop at the grass. Cautiously she stepped past the stones into the circle. She held on to her leather bag with one hand, and her cat-o'-nine-tails with the other.

A strange feeling ran through her. The air seemed thick with energy, and Ria licked her lips nervously. The magic locked into the stones was ancient and powerful. But she'd come too far to turn back now.

Time to get to work...

She tucked her cat-o'-nine-tails into

her belt, then strode to the nearest stone. She pulled handfuls of moss and dirt away from it. Underneath the muck were strange carvings: swirls and symbols, etched into the stone centuries ago.

Soon I'll have my revenge, Ria told herself with glee. *Soon I'll be rid of Tom…for ever!*

INTO THE PAST

"I don't understand," said Tom. He frowned at the chests, piled up all around the treasury and brimming with glittering treasure. "There's enough gold and silver here to sink a galleon…but Ria didn't touch any of it!"

Aduro raised an eyebrow. "There are more valuable things here than gold and silver, Tom. You know that."

Daltec had called his old master at once. Now the pair of them were sifting through the treasury, checking that everything was still in place after the raid.

"She must have taken something," said Elenna, who'd joined them from the walls, and was counting sacks of gold. "And whatever it is, she went to a lot of trouble to get it."

"You're not to blame," Harkman murmured to the shivering guard, still dressed in his underclothes. "She fooled us all."

The poor man sat hunched against the wall of the treasury, holding his head in his hands. *He must feel awful*, thought Tom. *It was his job to guard this place!*

As he looked past the man, his eyes fell on a dusty leather chest lying in the shadows. There were finger-marks on its lid. He walked over, and dragged the chest into the light. "Someone has touched this recently," he said.

The others crowded round. Taking off the lid, Tom reached in and pulled out a threadbare brown tunic. He passed it to Daltec. Then he brought out a cracked old belt, and last of all a worn-out boot, thickly coated with dust. The clothes smelled damp and musty, as though they hadn't been touched in years.

"What is all this?" asked Tom.

Aduro looked grave. "If I'm not mistaken," he said, "these objects

belonged to your predecessor, Tom. The very first Master of the Beasts."

"Tanner," said Elenna.

Tom's heart was thumping. "There's only one boot here," he said. "Do you think Ria took the other one?"

"A single boot?" Captain Harkman

frowned. "Why would anyone want to steal a smelly old shoe?"

"And where was she taking it?" said Daltec.

"Oh, no…" mumbled Aduro. His face had gone pale, and his hands trembled. "She headed south-east, you said?"

Elenna nodded.

"Then we've no time to lose," said Aduro. "We must travel to the Misty Glen at once."

Tom had heard of the place, growing up, because it was near to the village of Errinel. His uncle Henry had always warned him to stay away, because it was easy to get lost in the fog. "There's nothing there but a boggy valley," he said.

"I'm afraid there *is* something there," said Aduro. "Something far more dangerous than a bog. It's been hidden for centuries. But I fear that Ria has uncovered it."

"What is it?" said Elenna, frowning.

"A stone circle," said Aduro. "A place of powerful, ancient magic, built by the sorcerer Rufus. Ria could use it to do something extraordinary: to *travel through time*."

A hushed silence fell in the treasury. Tom swallowed hard. A cold dread was swirling in his stomach. *What is she planning?*

"And does the boot have something to do with it?" asked Captain Harkman.

"Ah, yes," said Aduro. "The boot

will take her back to the time it was in use. In this case, to the days when Tanner was Master of the Beasts. And whatever she does in that ancient time will affect the future – *this* future."

Tom didn't need to hear any more. *We can't let her destroy Avantia's past...* "I'll saddle Storm," he said.

Daltec shook his head. "I can get us there faster with magic." The wizard lifted his hands, and a blue light began to glow at the tips of his fingers. "Get ready, all of you..."

A moment later, Tom stumbled on to uneven, grassy ground. A cold wind cut through his tunic and made him shiver.

Glancing around, he saw Elenna next to him, rubbing her head. Daltec was there too, and Aduro. The old man was staring, wide-eyed, at something beyond...

Turning, Tom saw that they stood in a valley with grassy slopes rising on all sides. A chilly fog hung in the air. Then he spotted something through the mist. *The stone circle.* Nine rough-hewn columns of rock, arranged around a low stone altar.

Ria was striding from stone to stone, laying a palm on each one in turn and muttering under her breath. Peering closer, Tom saw that there were strange symbols carved on each rock. And as Ria touched them, the symbols began to glimmer like liquid gold...

"The stones," gasped Elenna suddenly. "They're shaking!"

She's right. The rocks were trembling, like dragon eggs about to hatch.

Heart pounding, Tom drew his sword and charged down the hillside. "Ria!" he called. But as he came close to the stone circle, his pace slowed. The air seemed to get thicker. *It's like wading through treacle!* Tom tried to force himself onwards, but soon he couldn't move a muscle. He stopped, panting and helpless.

"It's a magical shield!" cried Daltec, his voice full of despair.

"Your pet wizard is right," sneered Ria, as she laid her hand on the last stone. "Hello there, Tom. Or should I

say, goodbye?" Cackling, she walked to the middle of the circle, where Tom saw Tanner's boot sitting on a slab of rock.

Tom pushed, heaving with all his strength against the magical shield... but he couldn't get any closer.

Ria laid both hands on the altar. The last thing Tom saw was her horrible smirk. Then, with a sound like a clap of thunder, she vanished.

4

ERRIN'S HALL

Thunder rolled in Ria's ears. There was light everywhere, blinding bright, and she squeezed her eyes shut. Her stomach lurched as she fell, faster and faster, until suddenly her feet were resting on solid ground.

She opened her eyes.

The stone circle was gone. Instead there were just trees, rising all around. The sun shone down, and the branches threw twisting shadows across the ground. Birds twittered overhead.

A forest…

A pair of grazing goats looked up at her in alarm, bleated and scampered off into the darkness of the woods.

A slow smile spread across Ria's face. This was the same place she had been standing, moments before. *But… different.* She remembered the boot, and the altar she'd been touching. Both had vanished.

No matter – they had done their job. *Who would dream that an old boot could carry me four hundred years back in time?*

Ria let a chuckle escape her lips. Of course there were no standing stones in this age. The sorcerer Rufus hadn't built them yet. She remembered the tale her mother had told her – how Rufus had created the circle so that he might go back in time, to see his dead wife once more. *What a fool!* He never guessed what a powerful weapon he had made, or who might eventually use it...

But there would be time for celebration later. First, she had work to do.

She set off, walking along the bottom of the valley with the wooded slopes rising on either side of her. The trees thinned, and it wasn't long before she caught sight of smoke rising in the distance. *A settlement?* Ria changed direction, heading straight towards it.

She hadn't got far before she heard a yell from among the trees ahead.

"Who goes there?"

Ria raised her hands and stepped cautiously through the long grass. "Friend!" she called.

A thin, long-haired woman emerged from behind a tree. She was dressed in rags the colour of mud, and a necklace of animal teeth rattled around her neck. She clutched a bone-tipped spear in one hand.

The woman stared at Ria with wild eyes, then beckoned behind her. An older woman and a man rose from hiding places behind a thick bush, both dressed in the same way. The man had a baby tucked into an animal-skin

sling, and the woman held two young children by the hands.

"Who are you?" demanded the woman with the spear.

Ria shrugged. "Just a weary traveller, looking for a place to rest."

"Best turn away then," said the

woman, with a snort. "Errin's Hall is no place to rest. The village is under attack."

"I saw it," said one of the children. Her eyes were wide with terror. "It's a b-b-b—"

"Beast?" said Ria. Her heart was thumping.

"That's right," said the woman with the spear. "The foulest creature I've ever seen. We've summoned Tanner to fight it. Until then, we're hiding here in the woods. Join us, if you like."

Tanner... It was all Ria could do not to punch the air in triumph. *I've come just in time!*

"I fear no Beast," said Ria.

The woman blinked. "Are you mad, traveller?"

But Ria was already off, hurrying through the trees towards the village called Errin's Hall.

It wasn't long before she could hear the screams, and the terrified lowing of cattle. She ran towards the sounds, weaving between the trees. At last she stumbled out of the wood and saw the village, a cluster of simple stone buildings with log roofs, nestled at the bottom of the valley.

But there was no sign of a Beast. In fact, the place looked abandoned. *The pitiful peasants must be cowering in their homes*, she realised.

A deafening screech rent the air, and Ria's blood froze in her veins.

Something came surging up from behind the largest of the buildings. A creature as big as a house itself. Its body was armoured with scales, each one a sickly yellow-brown colour. Its wings stretched like sails on either side, throwing a shadow across the village. It circled once, then swooped down to perch on the roof of the large building.

Ria's heart pounded as she gazed at the Beast. Its head was hideously long and bristled with menacing blue spines. Its jaws were like a crocodile's and the edges of its wings were tipped with more sharp spines.

Petorix! Ria had read about this Beast in the *Chronicles of Avantia*. But she had never dreamed how large

the creature would be in the flesh. *Or how horrifying...*

A long, forked tongue flicked between Petorix's deadly teeth. Then she let out another piercing screech and began to tear at the roof with hooked talons. The wooden logs cracked and creaked as the Beast ripped them away and tossed them to the ground.

Ria savoured the screams of the villagers inside the building. Then she saw a cow charging wildly past on the ground below. Petorix whipped out her long tail, curling it around the animal. Then with a savage flick, she tossed it up into the air and snatched it in her jaws. Her throat bobbed as she gulped the cow down.

Ria's jaw dropped. *She swallowed it whole!*

Petorix lowered her head. Ria was sure she was about to dive through the gaping hole she had torn in the roof and devour the villagers. But instead she took off, flapping her wings and making a strange, cawing sound like a raven.

What has she seen?

Sheltering her gaze from the sun, Ria spotted something on the horizon. A speck, getting larger and larger as it swooped towards the village. It was a gigantic bird, with a curved beak and wings that seemed to blaze with fire.

Ria ducked down behind a fallen tree trunk. *Epos the Flame Bird.*

And now she saw something else.

A figure, perched on the giant bird's back, clinging on tightly to her feathers. A man dressed in a tough leather jerkin, with long dark hair that streamed back in the wind.

Ria's heart quickened, and her fingers dug into the bark of the tree.

Tanner.

She had only seen him in pictures before, on dusty old tapestries or faded scrolls, but there was no mistaking him. His brow was set in a fierce frown as he drove Epos closer to the village.

He thinks this is just another Beast Quest, thought Ria. *He thinks he'll defeat Petorix, enjoy the gratitude of the villagers, then go home for a hero's feast.*

She smirked.

He has no idea how wrong he is!

5

A HERO'S DEATH

The instant Ria disappeared inside the stone circle, so did the magical shield that had been protecting her. Tom stumbled forward and sprawled on the grass.

"Are you all right?" called Daltec. But Tom was already scrambling to his feet. He rushed forward among the stones. They were still and silent now, and the golden light had faded from the strange inscriptions. The boot still sat on the altar, smoking gently.

Cautiously, Tom reached out to touch it. When he found it was cool, he picked it up and examined it. It looked just the same as its counterpart, and it offered no clue of where Ria might have gone.

"Has she really travelled into the past?" said Tom.

"I'm afraid so," said Aduro. "The magic happened exactly as Rufus wrote that it would."

Elenna clenched her fists in frustration. "So what now? We can't let her play havoc with Avantia's history."

"Indeed not," said Daltec. The wizard looked pale. "But how are we to stop her?"

"There might be a way that we can go back in time too," said Aduro. The old man's brows were knit in deep thought. "The magical energy of Tanner's boot here has been all used up. But if we could find another artefact from the same age – something as similar as possible…"

"The other boot!" said Tom, understanding. "Come on then, what are we waiting for? Back to the castle."

In a flash of blue light, they were standing back in the treasury. Tom felt a familiar dizziness and rubbed at his head. *I don't think I'll ever get used to that…*

Elenna was already digging around in the ancient leather chest. "Uh oh," she murmured.

"What do you mean?" asked Daltec.

"The boot," said Elenna. "It's

not here. In fact…nothing is." She emptied the chest on to the floor. A spider tumbled out and scuttled into the shadows, but that was all.

"Oh dear," sighed Aduro. "This is precisely why Rufus decided never to use the circle! Even the tiniest change to the past can cause huge, disastrous changes to the present."

"That doesn't sound good," muttered Tom.

"I don't understand, Master," said Daltec. "If the circle is so dangerous, why has it never been destroyed?"

Aduro tutted. "Far too risky," he said. "The magic there is deep and powerful. Who knows what horrors might be unleashed if the circle was tampered with?"

"Wait," said Elenna. "What if we use something else to travel back? There must be some jewellery in the palace, or some armour… Something that was made in Tanner's time."

"That won't do, I'm afraid," said Aduro. "We need something connected to Tanner himself. Otherwise we could end up miles – or even years – away from where Ria is now."

They all fell silent, thinking. Then at last, Tom spoke. "I think I might have an idea," he said slowly. It was so horrible, he almost didn't want to say it out loud. *But we have to stop Ria…* He took a deep breath. "The Gallery of Tombs."

"Tanner is buried there," breathed Elenna.

Daltec had gone from pale to white as a sheet. "Are you suggesting we use his...bones?"

Aduro nodded gravely. "I don't like it. But it's the best idea we've got. Follow me..."

They hurried through torchlit corridors and down flights of steps, winding their way deep beneath the castle.

The shadows were thick and dark in every corner as they stepped into the Gallery. A row of stone sarcophagi stretched out into the gloom.

Tom felt a chill creep over his skin as they arrived at Tanner's final resting place. But he steeled himself and slid the blade of his sword in beneath the lid. Together, he and Elenna prised up the stone and lifted it aside.

"Something's wrong," said Aduro, at once. The old man reached inside and carefully picked up the hero's skull. The bone was mottled, with a strange purple sheen. It looked as though it might flake away into dust at any moment.

"What could have caused that?" wondered Daltec.

Even in the darkness, Tom could sense Aduro's frown. "Poison," he said quietly.

There was a silence. Then Elenna shook her head. "But that doesn't make sense. Everyone knows that Tanner died after his fight with Koba, Ghoul of the Shadows."

"Did he?" said Aduro. "Don't forget,

Ria's actions are changing the past. The history we know might not be true any more."

"So now Tanner died of poisoning?" said Tom.

Aduro nodded. "And not just any poison. There's only one that could have damaged his bones like this. A poison belonging to a certain Beast – one that he defeated. Or at least, one that he *had* defeated. Before Ria went into the past."

"Enough talk," said Tom. "Let's get after her." He bent to pick up the lid, and Elenna helped him slide it back into position.

But as they did so, Daltec gasped. "The inscription!"

They all peered at the words carved into the stone. "*Slain in his twentieth year*," Elenna read out loud. She frowned. "That's not right either! He was at least fifty, wasn't he?"

Aduro sank down on to a stone

bench. "She's done so much damage already," he said. "It might be too late…"

"But if there's even a chance of stopping her, we have to take it," said Tom. "Send us back in time. While there's blood in my veins, I'll bring that pirate to justice!"

POISON

Ria gasped to see the Beasts meet in mid-air, with a clash of talons and a thunder of flapping wings. The battle cries of Epos mingled with the wild screeches of Petorix, as the creatures tore and slashed at each other.

She watched Tanner carefully as he clung on to his gigantic steed's back. The hero had unslung a shield from his shoulders. He sheltered behind it as Petorix's deadly tongue flickered out and struck the wood, full on, with the weight of a metal flail. Ria could hear the *thwack*, even from so far below, and grinned.

Petorix's tongue was dripping with deadly, venomous saliva.

According to the *Chronicles of Avantia*, Tanner would soon leap from Epos's back on to Petorix. Then he'd draw his sword and sever the Beast's head with a single blow.

Time to rewrite history, thought Ria.

She saw Tanner stroke Epos's neck, whispering low by the bird's head. Then Epos banked upwards, wings beating the air as she soared above Petorix.

It's happening, Ria realised. *Any*

moment now, Tanner's going to jump!

Heart pounding, she vaulted over the fallen tree and dashed to the edge of the village. As she ran she muttered a spell under her breath, and she felt her hands getting hot. Purple light sprang from her fingertips, and she shaped the magic, moulding it into a twitching ball. Then she threw out her arms, hurling the missile up into the air.

It arced through the sky like a purple comet.

At the same instant, Tanner swung a leg over and launched himself off Epos's back. Down he plunged, feet first, straight towards Petorix…

Thump! The projectile slammed into him, like a rock from a catapult.

Ria caught a brief, delicious glimpse of his face – mouth open, eyes wide with shock – as the bolt knocked him off course. His limbs flailed madly. Then he plummeted straight past the Beast, towards the cold, hard ground.

It's over, thought Ria, in a rush of triumph. Epos wheeled in the air, squawking with panic, but there was nothing she could do. There was a cracking sound as Tanner plunged straight through the flimsy roof of a barn at the edge of a village, and a sickening *thud* from within.

Then silence.

Cheated of her prey, Petorix cawed. She flapped her wings and lashed her tail in fury.

Heart thumping, Ria darted in

among the little stone houses, heading for the barn. She couldn't stop grinning. *Who would have thought it would be so easy to kill him?*

When she reached the barn, she ran in through the open doors and skidded to a halt. The stone floor was strewn with hay, and hay bales were stacked in piles at the far end of the building, reaching almost to the rafters in places.

Then she heard a soft groan, and her gaze flicked to one side.

Tanner was sprawled on top of a low heap of bales. His hair had fallen across his face and bits of hay stuck to his clothes, but he was still breathing. *The hay must have broken his fall...* Slowly he rolled off and slumped to the floor. He heaved himself up on his knees and shook his head, looking dazed.

Ria scowled. *Let's finish the job.* Glancing around, she spotted a set of tools dangling from pegs by the doorway. She darted over, selected a curving bronze sickle and tested it with a finger. The blade was sharp.

Tanner hadn't seen her yet. She tiptoed over, raising the sickle…

Crack! Ria's boot crunched on a bit of broken wood from the roof. Tanner tensed. *Whhhshh!* Ria swung the sickle, but Tanner threw himself to one side and fell on the stone floor. "Who are you?" grunted Tanner, staring up at Ria.

Ria stalked towards him, raising the

sickle for a second blow. "Can't you just die?" she growled.

And at that moment darkness fell across the barn.

Glancing up, Ria felt her heart leap into her throat. Petorix loomed overhead, talons digging into the broken roof. The Beast's head was cocked, and her horrible forked tongue flickered across her bill.

Then she lunged, forcing her whole head through the hole in the roof and sending more bits of timber showering down.

Ria stumbled backwards.

Tanner looked up, and Ria saw his eyes widen with shock...

The Beast's deadly tongue shot out like a spear. Its twin forks stabbed

down, puncturing Tanner's jerkin and
plunging deep into his shoulder. Ria
gasped. Tanner's face had frozen in a
mask of horror.

Whumph! The barn lit up with a flash of orange, as a ball of fire struck Petorix. The Beast's tongue curled back into its mouth, and Tanner slumped to the ground. Petorix drew back her head, squealing in agony as flames burst across her body.

It's Epos, Ria realised. She hurled herself down behind a hay bale.

Still howling, Petorix took flight from the top of the barn. One of her wings was on fire, smoke billowing into the sky as she disappeared from view.

Ria was just about to stand when another shadow fell across the barn. With a gust of air, Epos swooped down through the hole in the roof. Her talons closed around the body of Tanner. Ria saw that the hero was utterly limp, like a sack of potatoes.

The Beast squawked once. Then she rose again, wings beating the air. Up she surged, through the hole in the roof. And as quickly as she'd come, she was gone again, carrying her master with her.

Ria stood at last. She felt shaky, and she leaned on a hay bale to support herself. But as her heart rate slowed, a smile spread across her face.

Tanner might have escaped. He might even still be alive. But he wouldn't be for long. Already, the poison of Petorix would be coursing through his blood.

You're going to die, Tanner. It's only a matter of time…

FORGOTTEN

"Let's hope Daltec hurries," said
Elenna, nervously. "The sooner we can
find Ria, the better."

Tom nodded. The young wizard had
gone straight from the crypt to find
the *Chronicles of Avantia*. According
to Aduro, the *Chronicles* might
already have changed, to reveal how
it was that Tanner had died so young.

Tom's fingers gripped the leather

bag that held Tanner's skull. He couldn't quite believe he was holding it. But as strange and as horrible as it was, he knew they had no choice if they were going to stop Ria.

"Captain Harkman, sir!" called a guard, marching over. "Reporting for duty." Tom recognised him as the dark-haired man who had been guarding the treasury.

"Back in uniform, then?" said Tom.

But instead of replying, the guard just saluted at Harkman.

"You can answer the Master of Beasts," Captain Harkman told the man. He gestured at Tom.

The guard frowned. "Answer who?"

Tom and Harkman looked at each other, puzzled. *Is he trying to be rude?*

"Now look here…" Harkman began. But he stopped as Aduro raised a hand. The old man's eyes were wide, and he was trembling with anxiety.

"Oh dear me," said Aduro. "I think I understand. Soldier – can you see anyone there?" He pointed at Tom.

The man was puzzled. "Er…no, sir."

"Just as I feared." Aduro laid his hands on Tom's shoulders. "I'm afraid that you are fading away. Your very *existence* is being erased."

"What?" exploded Elenna. "But he's right there!"

"The strongest connections will take the longest to sever," said Aduro. "Such as the one between you and Tom. But sooner or later, we will all lose him. We will forget that he ever existed – because he didn't."

Tom frowned. "I don't understand."

"This must have been Ria's plan all along," said Aduro. "If she has killed Tanner, as I fear, she did it so that Tom would never be born. If Tanner never had children, Tom would have no ancestors. He would never have existed."

Tom's head whirled. He clutched the skull tight, feeling as though he might be sick. *Ria's trying to destroy me*, he realised.

"Are you all right, Aduro?" said Harkman. He patted the old man on the back, smiling gently. "You do know you're talking to yourself?"

Elenna stared at Harkman in disbelief. "He's talking to Tom!" she said. "Can't you see?"

Harkman frowned. "Who's Tom?"

Tom shook his head. *This can't be happening!* He glanced down and froze. Something extraordinary was happening. He could see right through his arm to his boots. He lifted a hand and saw that it was see-through. *I'm turning into a ghost...*

"Where's Daltec?" he said. "We have to go back into the past, right now."

A small side door swung open, and the young wizard came scurrying out. His face was red, and he carried a fat leather-bound volume of the *Chronicles of Avantia* under one arm.

"Tom!" said Daltec, and Tom felt a rush of relief. *At least he's not forgotten me yet!*

"People can't see me any more," said

Tom, quickly. He didn't know how
long he had. "Ria's trying to erase me
from history, by killing Tanner."

"You have to get us to the stone
circle," said Elenna. "Quickly, Daltec.
Use your magic!"

Daltec blinked. "Us?" he said.

"Who's *us*?"

"Me and Tom!" cried Elenna.

Tom stepped forward and waved
a hand in front of Daltec's face. The
wizard didn't even react, and Tom felt
a cold weight in his belly. *Too late…*

"Just do it, my young friend," said
Aduro. "Take us to the Misty Glen."
He reached out for Tom's hand.
Elenna did the same.

Tom tucked the bag into his belt
and took their hands, gripping them
tight. *I can't disappear while I'm
holding on to them…can I?*

Daltec looked utterly baffled. But
to Tom's relief, the wizard finally
shrugged and laid down the book.
He lifted his hands, and a blue light
began to glow around the tips of

his fingers… In a flash, they were standing again by the stone circle.

Tom felt a rush of worry as Elenna and Aduro let go of his hands. But he knew he had a job to do. He tugged the bag from his belt, pulled out the skull and strode into the stone circle. Carefully he set the mottled piece of bone on the low altar in the middle.

"Very good," said Aduro. "Now you must go from stone to stone, and lay your palm on the correct symbols." He pointed to a swirling star shape on the nearest stone, and Tom went to place his hand on it.

"The skull will take you back in time," Aduro said, "but the magic won't last for ever. Sooner or later you will return here, to this circle."

If I still exist at all, thought Tom.

"I'm coming too," said Elenna. But Aduro held her back by the arm.

"I don't think that would be wise," he said. "If two people use the circle, the magic might go wrong."

"It's all right, Elenna," said Tom, as Aduro directed him to a symbol on the next stone. "I'll face Ria alone if I have to." Elenna frowned, but she allowed Aduro to hold her in place.

As Tom touched more stones, he saw that the symbols were glimmering with a shifting golden light. *Just like when Ria travelled back in time.* He felt a strange lightness, as though his body was made of air. He couldn't tell if it was the magic of the circle, or if he was about to disappear entirely.

With a lurch of fear, he hurried to touch the symbol on the final stone.

As his fingers left it, the symbols seemed to glow even brighter than before. The stones trembled, ready to unleash their magic...

Tom looked out and saw that a mystical haze had formed around the circle, as though he were looking at the world from inside a giant bubble.

"What now?" he called.

But Aduro didn't answer. "Dear me, Elenna," he said. "For the life of me, I can't remember why we came here."

Oh no... Fear gripped Tom.

"Elenna!" he called, his voice breaking. "What do we do now?"

Elenna locked her gaze on his, and he couldn't mistake the grim

determination in her eyes.

"This," she said.

Before Tom could stop her, she
threw off Aduro's arm and ran into
the circle. Snatching Tom by both
hands, she pulled him along, and set
all four of their hands on the skull.

STORY TWO

Alas for Tanner… The boldest of warriors, so cruelly slain!

Deep in his fortress, he lay stricken on his wooden bier. For three days and three nights he writhed, as the poison of Petorix devoured him from within. His faithful friends watched him waste away: noble Gwen, fiery Castor and wise Rufus. They sought to save him, but no potion could soothe his suffering.

On the fourth day, brave Tanner closed his eyes for the last time. His bones were clear for all to see, purple and spotted through his pale, papery skin.

High up on the ramparts, loyal Firepos mourned. She shrieked out her grief, in honour of the suffering her master had endured.

Extract from *The Chronicles of Avantia*

SORCERY!

A searing heat rushed up through Tom's arms. The world shuddered, the vibrations jangling every bone in his body. *It's like I'm being ripped apart!*

Then, with a crack of thunder, the strange sensations were gone, and he stood on solid ground.

"Whoa," breathed Elenna.

Tom blinked and saw her beside him, gazing about in awe.

They were in a sun-dappled forest clearing. Silence reigned, except for the twittering of the birds. *We did it! We went back in time...*

Tom licked his lips nervously. "Elenna?" he said. "Can you see me?"

Elenna grinned at him. "Clear as day. Looks like escaping to the past has put a stop to your disappearing act."

Tom felt a wave of relief rush over him. "We'd better get after Ria," he said. "Aduro said the magic of the stone circle won't last. We have to find her, before the spell wears off and we go back to our own time."

They were just about to set out when a little girl shot from the undergrowth. She wore a tunic made from deer hide, and her wrists rattled with bone bracelets. "Bandits!" she screeched.

More people emerged from among the trees: a dozen men, women and children, all dressed in animal hides. Some of them had sacks slung over their shoulders, stuffed to bursting. They were all streaked with ash.

"It's all right!" Tom called. "We're not bandits."

The little girl clung to the legs of an old, bearded man with short grey hair. He gently detached himself and shuffled forwards. "You look like warriors," he said, eyeing Tom's weaponry. "If only you had come sooner…"

"What do you mean?" asked Elenna.

"Our village was attacked," said an old woman, her voice trembling. "The

Beast Petorix laid waste to it. Errin's Hall is no more!"

Errin's Hall… Tom gasped. *That must be what Errinel was called four hundred years ago!*

"We can help you," said Elenna, stepping forward. "Tom here is the Master of the Beasts."

The villagers looked puzzled.

"We don't understand," said the old man, politely. "Tanner is Master here."

"Or at least, he was," muttered the old woman.

Tom's blood ran cold. "What do you mean, *was*? He's not… Is he…"

"Dead?" finished Elenna.

"He lives, but not for long," said the old woman, her face grave. "He fell in battle with Petorix, and lies dying at his fortress."

Tom swallowed hard. Then he noticed that the old woman's arm was in a rough sackcloth sling. "Let us help with that, at least," he said.

Drawing the green jewel from his belt, he stepped closer and laid it on the old woman's arm.

She flinched at first, her brow knitting with alarm. Then she froze as the jewel began to glow. Tom knew its healing magic would be spreading through her arm like cool water.

When he stepped away, the old woman flexed her arm and gasped. A murmur ran among the villagers.

"Sorcery!" breathed the old man. He looked at Tom and Elenna, eyes gleaming. "Perhaps you might be able

to help Tanner with your magic."

A tall villager stepped out from
among the trees, leading a sleek
black charger with a shining mane.
"Midnight is our fastest horse," he
said. "But you shall have him, for the

sake of Tanner."

Tom bowed low. "Thank you," he said. "And don't worry. We'll save the Master of the Beasts."

"There it is!" cried Elenna, as they reached a hilltop.

Tom twitched the reins, and Midnight reared to a halt. The horse snorted, his flanks damp with sweat.

The sun had begun to sink through the sky as they rode. Midnight had carried them out of the forest, across meadows and over hills. Now they finally had the City within sight. *Or at least, the place that will one day be the City*, thought Tom.

"It looks…different," he said.

Tanner's fortress was built out of wooden logs on a low hillock below them. Attached to it, extending on to the lower slopes, was a wooden-fenced enclosure full of small buildings. *The City's not much more than a village in this age!* thought Tom. There was no trace of the high stone walls of King Hugo's palace, or the proud blue banners of Avantia flying from the turrets.

"Come on," said Elenna. "We can get there before sunset."

They galloped down the hillside and across the fields to the village. The wooden gates stood wide open, and they slowed to a trot as they passed through.

Villagers bustled among the little

houses, chopping up wood, feeding goats and cooking over open fires. But they all stopped to look up with curiosity as Tom and Elenna passed. Chickens pecked in the dirt. At the far side of the village, a flight of stone steps were set into the hillside, leading up to the wooden fortress above. Tom and Elenna made their way over, then dismounted and tied Midnight to a hitching post.

Side by side, they began to climb.

The doors to the fortress were very tall and covered in carvings of Beasts. Tom recognised the sweeping wings of Epos around the door handles. Taking a deep breath, he rapped hard.

After a while, they heard footsteps inside. Then one of the doors creaked open a little way. A young man with a mop of blond hair peered out. "What do you want?" he demanded.

The man had piercing blue eyes and jutting cheekbones. His lips were curled in an arrogant sneer.

"Who is it?" asked someone from inside. Tom saw it was a woman the same age, with snow-white hair tied back from her delicate face.

"We're here to help Tanner," said Tom.

The blond man snorted. "You can't be serious? You're just children."

"We're heroes, actually," said Elenna, glaring at him.

"*Actually*," said the blond man, "you're wasting our time. Run along home now."

He stepped back and pulled the

door to. But Tom slipped his boot inside, stopping the door.

The blond man snarled. "Perhaps you didn't hear me?" He laid a hand on the golden hilt of a sword that hung from his belt.

"Leave them be, Castor," said the white-haired woman, softly.

Tom's heart lurched. *Castor! From the* Chronicles of Avantia…

"Wait a second," said Elenna, her eyes wide with astonishment. "If you're Castor…" She turned to the white-haired woman. "Then you must be Gwen! We've read about you both."

A smug smile spread across Castor's face. "Well, I'm certainly well-known round these parts."

And just as arrogant as the

Chronicles *recorded*, thought Tom. He bit his lip, then did his best to smile. "You're friends of Tanner, aren't you? So let us help him. Please?"

Castor scowled. "I've had enough of your insolence." He slammed the door open wide and stepped outside.

Tom backed away. His hand closed on his own sword hilt.

"I'd leave that alone, little boy," said Castor. "Don't want you slicing your own hand off, do we? I'm just going to teach you some manners." He rolled up the sleeves of his tunic, and curled his fingers into fists.

Tom's gaze flicked to the open door behind Castor. *Now's my chance...*

Ducking low, he darted forward, feeling a whistle of air as Castor

swung a fist, too high. Then he drove
the edge of his shield down hard on
to Castor's boot. Castor doubled up,
grunting with pain.

As Tom dashed for the door, he

heard Elenna gasp. "Look out!"

Out of the corner of his eye, Tom saw a flash of orange. He spun, and his eyes went wide.

Something had dropped from a rampart overhead, landing squarely on four huge paws.

It was a giant cat, with flame-coloured fur and yellow eyes that glared hungrily at Tom. Its back arched, and it let out a soft hiss.

"You've done it now," grunted Castor. He was hopping up and down, holding on to his injured foot. "Meet Nera. You know, it's been a while since she's tasted human flesh."

Of course... Tom remembered now what he'd read in the *Chronicles*. Each of Tanner's companions had a loyal Beast of their own.

Elenna stepped up beside Tom, fitting an arrow to her bow… But before she could raise it, a shadow fell over them and a second Beast came swooping out of the sky to land at Nera's side. This one was a grey wolf, with giant wings like a bat's. It folded them, watching calmly.

"And this is Gulkien," said Gwen, from the doorway. "I suggest you lay your weapons down now."

Tom saw Elenna's knuckles go white as she gripped her bow, ready to fight. "We can't," he whispered. "We mustn't make enemies here."

"It might be too late for that," said a new voice.

A man in long red robes stepped

out of the fortress. His hair was the
colour of fire. *Rufus!* thought Tom.

The young wizard threw out a hand.
Scarlet smoke coiled from his fingers
and swirled around Tom and Elenna,
tugging them towards each other.

Tom struggled, but the smoke was
magically solid and strong as iron. He
and Elenna were both held tight.

"Well, this *has* been enjoyable,"
sneered Castor. "But now, I'm afraid,
it's time for us to throw you in the Pit."

2

NOTHING PERSONAL

Out in the fields, a lonely, hunched figure hobbled her way towards Tanner's fortress. Night had fallen, and a chill wind blew across the field.

Ria shivered and pulled her cloak tighter around her, making sure her face was hidden by the hood. She had taken it from a cowardly merchant driving a cart of apples towards Errin's

Hall. He'd taken one look at her cat-o'-nine-tails and offered her whatever she wanted. *Just a cloak, and a little information...*

Ria gritted her teeth in frustration. Tanner really should have died by now. But according to the merchant, he was still clinging desperately to life. *His pet sorcerer Rufus must be keeping him alive, somehow.*

This time, Ria swore, she would make sure the job was finished.

To cheer herself up, she thought of Tom. By now he must have figured out her plan – to kill Tanner, so that he would never be born. She couldn't imagine how terrified he would be, as he slowly disappeared. *And there's nothing he can do about it!*

How would poor Elenna cope without her best friend?

How would the kingdom survive, with no Master of the Beasts to protect it?

The thoughts warmed Ria's heart.

"Halt! Who goes there?"

Ria flinched at the cry. She had reached the village below the fortress, and she saw a guard standing at the gate, clutching a spear.

"Just a poor old woman," she croaked, trying to make herself sound as feeble as possible. "Looking for shelter, and a crust to chew on."

The guard nodded, and Ria passed on through.

Silently she made her way among the peasant hovels, keeping away from the glowing warmth of the fires inside, and sticking to the darkness. She climbed the steps towards the fortress, silent as a shadow herself.

As she reached the top, she felt under her cloak for her cat-o'-nine-tails, and a slender dagger she'd tucked into her belt. The main doors were shut, but Ria skirted around the edge of the fortress to where the shadows were darkest. The wooden logs that made up the walls were rough and pitted with axe marks. Ria lost no time in scaling one, clinging tight as she hauled herself up, then vaulted over the top.

Thump! She landed softly in the courtyard of packed earth within.

Glancing around, she soon saw the

flickering glow of a fire coming from
a half-open door. She crept towards it
and peered inside.

It was a small room with a hearth,
and thick furs spread on the floor. Ria's
throat went dry as she saw Tanner,
lying flat on a wooden bier in the
middle of the room.

Cautiously, she stepped through the door. Tanner didn't move a muscle. His skin was white, Ria saw, and covered in a sheen of sweat. His eyes were glazed and his eyelids flickered, as though he were in the middle of a bad dream.

It can't be as bad as what's about to happen, thought Ria. Smirking, she drew the dagger from her belt. All she had to do was slide it into his heart.

She lifted the blade, gripping the hilt.

She hesitated. *Killing a defenceless man...* It almost felt...wrong.

Tanner's eyelids snapped open. He stared up at Ria, and suddenly she saw the resemblance. *He's Tom's ancestor. Tom, my mortal enemy.*

Ria drove the knife down.

Tanner grunted and grasped her

wrist. The knife point hovered above his chest, brought up short.

"No," he gasped.

Ria could feel how weak he was. Just one more shove, and it would all be over. She grinned down at him. "If it makes you feel better," she whispered, "it's nothing personal."

She lent her weight to the hilt, pushing it down.

"Stop!"

Ria spun round at the sudden shout. A young man stood in the doorway, wearing robes the colour of blood, his hair fiery red. He threw out a hand, and a ruby-red bolt shot from his palm.

Ria yelped in shock as the bolt struck her hand, sending the knife spinning.

"Falkor!" called the man. And from

above Ria's head there came a soft, hissing sound.

Hardly daring to breathe, Ria looked upwards. Her heart stopped.

Coiled around a wooden beam, just above her, was an enormous snake. It had to be as long as a ship's mast was tall, and its scales gleamed black in the firelight.

A forked red tongue flickered from its mouth. Then, in one sudden movement, it descended, coiling around her body. Ria was paralysed with fear. The snake squeezed at her, holding her firmly in its grip.

"I've caught an assassin," said the red-haired man.

It took Ria a moment to realise he wasn't talking to her. A white-haired

woman had stepped into the room.

The newcomer nodded grimly.
"Another one," she said. "Very well. She
can join the others."

1

3

FIREPOS

Tom laid a hand on the nearest wall.
It was cold earth, scraped smooth. *No
way to climb up.* Moonlight filtered
through the gaps in the metal grid
above, and Tom could just make
out Elenna's eyes gleaming in the
darkness beside him. *There isn't even
enough space for us to lie down in
here!*

He cupped his hands and called

upwards. "You're making a big mistake! Let us out, so we can help Tanner."

A shadow fell over them, as the silhouette of a face appeared at the grid. "I wouldn't waste your breath, if I were you," said Castor, in his arrogant drawl.

He took a big bite of an apple, then dropped the core through a gap in the grid.

"Hey!" snapped Elenna, as the core bounced off her shoulder.

Castor just laughed.

"If you just take my shield," tried Tom, lifting it up. "There's a magical token set into the wood. A phoenix's talon... It could cure Tanner!"

Castor hesitated. But when he spoke,

Tom could hear the suspicion in his voice. "What's a dirty farm boy like you doing with magical tokens?"

Tom fought down a fresh surge of frustration. "I'm not a farm boy," he said, as patiently as he could. "That's what I've been trying to tell you. I'm Master of the Beasts!"

"Ha!" Castor shook his head. "Well, you're funny. I'll give you that."

"So-called heroes..." muttered Elenna. "I can't believe I was excited to meet them!"

"Castor." It was Gwen's voice. Tom could hear her footsteps, as she approached the top of the pit. "We've caught another one."

Tom and Elenna exchanged a glance. *Another one?* Tom's stomach squirmed with unease.

"Well, what a treat," said Castor. Metal squealed as he opened the grid.

Tom heard the sounds of a scuffle, voices raised and boots pounding the earth. Then a shadowy bulk came hurtling down into the pit…

"Look out!" squawked Elenna.

Tom threw himself to one side, just in time.

Thump! The new prisoner hit the ground. At once she was scrabbling to her feet, but the metal grid had already slid shut.

With a lurch of his heart, Tom recognised her.

"Ria!" he gasped.

The pirate girl's eyes glittered with fury. A shaft of moonlight fell on her face, and Tom saw her lips curl into a sneer. "I should have known there'd be a few rats down here," she spat.

Tom felt rage flood his limbs, but
Elenna laid a hand on his arm. Tom
forced himself to stay calm. "You..."
he growled. "This is all your fault!"

Ria laughed bitterly. "Oh, is that
what you tell yourself? In case you've

forgotten, you killed my father, Sanpao. So I think it's only fair if I kill your great, great, great, great… whatever in return. And make sure you're never born."

"That's nonsense," snapped Elenna. "Tom didn't kill Sanpao. That pirate got himself killed by the Beast, Verak!"

"Well, this has been entertaining," came Castor's voice, from above. Tom looked up to see the young man smirking down at them. "But I'm afraid I have more important things to attend to than the ravings of madmen. Sleep tight now, and mind the cockroaches don't bite." He stood, chuckling, and strode away.

Stuck in here with our worst enemy,

thought Tom, clenching his fists.

A savage smile spread across Ria's face. "I wonder if Tanner is actually dead yet?" she said. "He must be growing weaker and weaker, with every breath he takes."

"Ignore her, Tom," said Elenna.

But Tom was hardly listening. He was watching the moonlight glint off the talon set in his shield. *I think I might have an idea...*

Heart racing, Tom lifted his shield and placed the talon against the ruby-red jewel in his belt. Then he closed his eyes, drawing the magic deep inside him.

Epos, he thought. *Are you there? Can you hear me?*

At first there was nothing. Tom

frowned. Of course, the Epos in this time wasn't the same as the one he had befriended.

Then a thought struck him. According to the *Chronicles*, Epos wasn't always called that. She had a longer name, centuries before. *Perhaps if I called her by that name...?*

Tom screwed his eyes tight shut. He concentrated as hard as he could. *Firepos*, he said with his mind. *Come to me. If you can hear me, it proves I am a friend of Tanner's. We need your help!*

"What's he doing?" said Ria. "He looks like he's lost his mind."

But before Elenna could answer, there was a beating of wings overhead, like sudden gusts of wind.

Tom's heart leapt. *Firepos!*

Darkness fell through the pit, as the Beast swooped from the sky and landed. There was a rustle of feathers, then a gleaming golden eye appeared above the grid, its night-black pupil as big as Tom's shield.

Ria's jaw dropped. "What on...?" she muttered.

"Has she come to help us?" murmured Elenna, gazing in wonder.

The eye disappeared. Then a giant yellow talon grasped hold of the grid. The metal groaned as Firepos tugged. With a *clang* it was gone, and the Beast tossed it aside.

A flame-coloured wing descended, gently, into the pit, and Tom understood. *She wants us to climb on!* Taking hold of the feathers, he hauled himself up the Beast's wing. He could hear Elenna climbing behind him.

"So you're going to leave me here, are you?" called Ria, from below.

"We're not taking you with us!" Elenna snapped back.

"It won't matter either way," crowed Ria. "It's too late for Tanner!"

Ignoring her taunts, Tom pulled himself out of the pit. The cold night air pressed his tunic against his body, chilling him to the bone. But he hauled himself up on to the Beast's back. Turning, he gave Elenna a hand as she settled herself behind him.

Go, Firepos, Tom said, speaking within his mind. *Fly!*

The Beast let out a screech. Then with a sudden rush of wind she lurched up into the sky. Her wings powered through the air. Tom glanced back and caught a glimpse of the pit, getting smaller and smaller below. Ria was already out of sight, hidden by the shadows. *Good riddance!*

They flew higher, swooping in a huge circle. Tom saw the fortress below, the wooden stockade and the cluster of houses on the slopes beneath it. *Down*, he thought, and Firepos dipped her wings. They glided lower, heading straight towards the courtyard of the fortress.

"Are you sure about this?" said Elenna, nervously.

"Not really," Tom admitted.

Firepos spread her wings wide as they landed with a jolt in the middle of the courtyard.

Tom slid to the ground, gripping his shield tightly.

A door swung open on the other

side of the courtyard. Rufus strode out, his red robes rippling in the wind. Tom was pleased to see the wizard's eyes widen as he took in the sight of Firepos, strutting and clawing at the dirt.

"Please," said Tom. "I'll ask you one more time. Let us help you."

Rufus gaped at him. Then slowly, he began to smile. "I think you've proved that you're more than capable," he said quietly. "Whoever you are, you clearly have a gift with Beasts."

"Let us heal Tanner then," said Tom.

But Rufus shook his head. "I wish it were so simple. I have exhausted my magic, and though he has managed to rise, the effect will not last long. He is too brave for his own good. There is only one cure for the poison that runs through Tanner's blood."

"Which is?" asked Elenna. She jumped down beside Tom.

"Egg shell," said Rufus, simply. "But not just any egg. The egg from which the foul Beast who poisoned him hatched. Petorix, the Winged Slicer."

"Where do we find the egg?" asked Tom.

"In the Beast's lair," said Rufus, gravely. "You will find it at the edge of the Hartswood. It's a great forest to the northwest. Castor and Gwen have just set out for it. But if you were to join them…"

"Don't worry, Rufus," said Tom, as bravely as he could. "We'll defeat the Beast…and we'll save Tanner's life!"

THE STUPIDITY OF HEROES

Ria aimed a kick at the earthen side of the pit, and pain spiked through her toe. *You're pathetic, Tom!* she thought, clutching furiously at her boot. *Getting mangy Beasts to do all your work for you…*

There was no time to lose. She couldn't be sure that Tanner had died yet. *And if I know Tom, he'll find a way to save the wretch!*

She tried to dig her fingertips into the sides of the pit. But the earth was cold and solid, and she couldn't get a grip. *No good.* She crouched, then leapt as high as she could, reaching for the top of the wall. *Not even close.*

Ria scowled. If only she could fly... Then she blinked. *Of course!*

Reaching inside her coat, she drew a small glass vial from a pocket. The small amount of purple liquid it held sparkled in the moonlight.

Ria held her breath as she uncorked it. She couldn't waste a single drop. It was the very last of her Floating Elixir. Once, she had powered whole fleets of flying ships with the magical fluid, but Tom had destroyed them all, together with the Elixir Wells on the island of Makai.

Grimacing, she tipped the vial and sprinkled the Elixir on to her boots.

At first, nothing happened. Then slowly, gradually, Ria felt herself lifting off the ground. *I'm flying*, she thought as she rose. *No pit can hold the mighty Ria!*

Reaching the top, she felt herself slowing. Her heart lurched, but she grasped the edge of the hole and hauled herself out on to the grass.

After the magic had worn off, she glanced cautiously around. The pit was in the little enclosure of houses, not far from the steps up to the fortress. It loomed over her, a dark shadow like a crouching Beast.

The peasants were all asleep and the settlement was silent. *No time to lose!*

Ria hurried up the steps. This time the fortress gates were wide open, and she darted through, crouching low and keeping to the shadows. The firelight still shone from Tanner's room, and she crept carefully to the window.

Peering inside, she was shocked to see Tanner on his feet. His face was pale as he buckled up his sword belt.

Rufus looked anxiously at Tanner. "You *must* rest," said the wizard.

Tanner shook his head. "I've already told you, Rufus. You can't stop me. It's my duty to face Petorix."

The stupidity of heroes, thought Ria.

She hesitated, frowning. Surely the poison would work soon. But there

was no harm in helping it along…

Grinning, Ria reached in through the window and lifted a flaming torch from its bracket.

"Intruder!" cried Rufus. The wizard flung out his hand. But before he could cast a spell, Ria tossed the torch on to the furs covering the floor.

Whoosh! Flames leapt up at once. Rufus stared in horror as the fire began to spread. In moments, thick black smoke had filled the room, hiding Rufus and Tanner from view.

Ria darted away. She snatched another torch from its bracket and tossed it to the base of the wooden wall. *That should keep them busy!*

At the gates, Ria paused. Tanner would be dead soon, whether from the poison or the fire. That would be the end of it. *But it would be so satisfying to kill Tom myself...*

She couldn't resist. She ran on, down the steps and into the settlement below. She followed her nose to a stable, untied the fittest-looking stallion and hopped up on his back.

The stallion took off, galloping out of the stable and through the night. The wind buffeted Ria's face. She caught a glimpse of the guard on the gate as she passed, his surprised face turning to look at her. But by then she was out, racing through the fields.

"Faster!" she yelled, kicking the horse's flanks cruelly. She glanced back, and saw that the fire she had set was spreading across the walls of the fortress. The blazing wooden building lit the night up like a beacon, belching black smoke into the sky.

Good luck escaping that, Tanner, she thought. Then she crouched low, driving the horse on. *I'm coming for you, Tom. This ends tonight!*

5

THE GIANT NEST

"There it is!" cried Elenna, pointing over Tom's shoulder. "The Hartswood."

Up ahead, the fields gave way to a mass of trees that spread into the distance like a dark ocean.

Tom frowned as Firepos swooped, carrying them closer. His eyes were streaming in the night air, and his fingers were numb from holding on tight to the giant Beast's feathers.

"Isn't that the Forest of Fear?" he said.

Elenna shrugged. "I suppose it must have got that name later on."

I wonder why, thought Tom. A prickle of dread crept down his spine.

A shadow rose suddenly from among the trees. Firepos squawked, and Tom's hand flew to his sword hilt. Then he saw that it was a wolf with bat wings, flapping madly as it cleared the trees.

"That's Gulkien!" said Elenna. "But he looks hurt."

Sure enough, Tom saw that the Beast's left wing was torn. Sprawled across Gulkien's back, dressed in a dark green cloak, was Gwen.

"Do you think she's alive?" whispered Elenna.

"No time to find out," said Tom. "We have to defeat Petorix."

Firepos spread her wings and they glided down, brushing through the leaves where Gulkien had taken off.

As the giant bird landed in the clearing, Elenna drew in a sharp breath. "And there's Castor," she said.

Tom peered into the shadows beneath the trees and spotted the blond-haired warrior lying on the ground. He was trapped under the huge bulk of his own Beast, Nera. The golden cat lay still, her eyes shut, her tongue lolling. To his horror, Tom saw a bright red wound stretching along the Beast's back.

"Petorix must be even more deadly than we thought," murmured Elenna.

Tom quickly slid to the ground and ran to Castor.

The warrior snarled up at him. "What are you...doing here...farm boy?" he grunted. He grimaced with pain, and

Tom saw that his hair was plastered to his head with sweat.

"We've come to defeat Petorix," said Elenna, joining Tom. "Looks like you could do with a hand."

Castor laughed bitterly. "You really...shouldn't have. That Beast... She's too powerful."

"Let's get him out," said Tom. He took one arm and Elenna took the other. "One...two...THREE!" Heaving with all their strength, they tugged Castor free from under Nera's bulk.

Castor groaned, and Tom saw why. "His legs are broken!" he said.

"Give me the green jewel," said Elenna. "I'll heal him. You go and deal with Petorix."

Tom took the jewel from his belt

and passed it to Elenna. Then he peered into the darkness of the trees.

"That way," grunted Castor, pointing. "You're brave, farm boy. I'll give you that."

Tom nodded goodbye to Elenna, hoping it wouldn't be for the last time. Then he set off, alone. He drew his sword, and held on tight to his shield. His heart was thumping.

The trees were sparse, and some of them were damaged, branches torn away or whole trunks ripped from the soil and leaning against other trees. *Petorix's work*, thought Tom.

The sky had begun to lighten as dawn approached. But there was no birdsong. No sound but the snapping of twigs underfoot, as Tom went deeper into the forest.

Up ahead, a shadowy shape became clearer as he wove between the trees. It was a mass of ripped-apart boughs and branches, as big as a house. The shape looked familiar. Then, with a prickling at the back of his neck, Tom realised why.

It's a nest! But far bigger than any bird's...

Tom froze, listening hard. But there was no sound. No trace of the Beast. Approaching cautiously, he put his sword away. Then he began to climb, hauling himself up through the branches until he reached the top and could see into the hollow within.

His eyes widened. There they were – shattered fragments of white shell,

each piece as big as a dinner plate.
The antidote... Tom half scrambled,
half slid down into the nest.
Snatching the nearest piece of shell,
he tucked it away inside his tunic.

He was just about to climb back
when the whole nest seemed to shift
beneath him. He spun around.

Petorix!

Tom's heart thundered. The Beast
that perched on the far edge of the
nest was vast – even bigger than
Firepos – with scales that looked dull
yellow in the pre-dawn light. She
stared at Tom with huge, reptilian
eyes, and cocked her head. The blue
spines bobbed, like a helmet's plume.

The Beast gave a sudden screech,
and swiped with a wing. Tom hardly

had time to notice its jagged edge, before instinct took over. He threw up his shield. *Thump!* The blow sent him tumbling across the nest.

Petorix swiped with her other wing, and this time Tom dodged, setting a boot on a branch and launching himself to one side. He was panting, heart racing. *I'm trapped in her nest!*

The Beast opened her crocodile jaws, and Tom saw her hideous tongue lashing out like a whip.

He fumbled his sword from its scabbard. But the Beast's tongue seized it and tugged hard, almost yanking Tom's arm from its socket.

Tom clung on to his sword hilt for all he was worth. The tongue had wrapped around the blade, and now

Petorix was hauling him in, like he was a fish on a line. He struggled, but the sword was caught tight.

Just when Tom thought the Beast's jaws would snap shut on his arm, Petorix spread her wings and beat the

air. To his astonishment, Tom found his boots leaving the nest. Petorix was dragging him up into the sky. *Where's she taking me?*

The Beast surged up through the branches of the trees, and the twigs and leaves lashed at Tom's face. He gasped for breath. Glancing down, he saw the canopy of the forest below, rapidly sinking away. He gasped. *If I fall now, I'm dead...*

But he could not hold on much longer. His palms were slick with sweat, and he was losing his grip on the sword. With a last, desperate lunge, he tried to grab Petorix's tongue instead. But it was slimy, and slid between his fingers. As he fell he knew this was it – the end.

CURSED AVANTIANS

Ria jerked the horse's mane, making it rear and stumble to a halt.

They had reached a clearing in the forest, and she could see something through the leafy canopy. A shadow, rising through the deep blue sky.

No – two shadows!

She squinted, peering closer. The larger creature was Petorix – she could tell from the curving arcs

of the Beast's wings. But there
was something – *someone* – else
too, hanging from the creature's
outstretched tongue.

Tom!

Ria watched in astonishment as the
Master of the Beasts struggled with
Petorix… then dropped like a stone
towards the forest. A savage smile
spread across her face. *Even Tom's no
match for that Beast.*

Then a pair of hands closed over
her left leg and tugged her from the
horse. Caught off guard, Ria fell into
the mud. She heard a frightened
neigh, and felt the ground shake
as her horse took off, disappearing
among the trees. *Worthless creature!*

She was just about to stand when a

boot pressed on to her chest, pinning her in place. A shadow fell over her, and she looked up to see Elenna glaring. The girl already had an arrow fitted to her bowstring, and it was pointing straight at Ria's neck.

Ria swallowed hard. "I don't know why you bother," she said, trying to sound relaxed. "It's not as if you're going to shoot."

"Try me," growled Elenna.

Ria laughed. "You're just too *good*, that's your trouble. Killing someone defenceless really isn't your style."

Elenna gripped her bow tightly.

"Anyway, you should probably check on Tom," said Ria, hastily. "Didn't you see him fall just now? I don't know how you'd cope without him…do you?"

Elenna's eyes flickered away for a moment, and Ria knew she'd won.

"I'm coming back for you," hissed Elenna. Then she lowered her bow and disappeared into the forest.

Ria leapt to her feet. With luck, the fall really had killed Tom. But she had to see for herself. She followed, striding after Elenna.

She had almost reached the edge of the clearing when something stirred nearby. A shadowy bulk, half-seen among the tree trunks.

Ria froze. *What was that?*

With a rustle of feathers, a Beast came tearing into the clearing. Its wings were half-folded, and its wide orange eyes gazed sternly at her.

Ria's mouth went dry. She took a step backwards. "Good birdie," she croaked. "Nice birdie."

Firepos prowled forward, her talons crunching leaves and twigs with each step. Without thinking, Ria reached for her cat-o'-nine-tails. But of course it wasn't there. *Cursed Avantians*, she thought. *Stealing my weapons!*

Firepos cocked her head. Then she gave a vicious squawk. Any moment now, Ria knew the Beast would lunge forward and swallow her whole...

"Enough, Firepos!"

Ria spun round at the sudden shout. *Tanner!* The young warrior came out of the gloom of the forest, riding another Beast. Ria gasped when she recognised it. It was the giant snake that had caught her in Tanner's chamber, its scales gleaming as its body wound among the tree trunks.

The wizard's Beast, thought Ria... *But where's the wizard?*

No sooner had she thought it, than a figure in red appeared at Tanner's side. Scarlet light glimmered at his fingertips, and he thrust out a hand. *Ffffzzaapp!* A bolt of magic lit up the forest and struck Ria.

She stumbled in shock, then realised she had felt no impact. But when she looked down, she saw the light coiling around her, forming itself into the thick links of a chain. She tried to move her arms, but the chains of light held her in place. She took a step forward and fell, as the chains wrapped around her legs as well as her arms.

Writhing on the ground, she snarled up at the hero, the wizard and the slithering serpent. "You're too late!" she crowed. "Tom's finished!"

HERE LIES A HERO

The leaves rustled as Tom dropped through them, hurtling towards the ground. He gritted his teeth. Any moment now, he would feel the sickening crunch of the impact…

Thump! Something struck his back, knocking him off course. He fell, twigs scratching at him, slowing him, until he was caught upside down, snagged on a branch by his ankle.

He shifted, blinking. He'd landed in a bush, not far from Petorix's nest. Glancing up, he saw the narrow branch he'd fallen on, still vibrating. If he hadn't hit it, he would have smashed on to the hard ground below. *That bit of wood saved my life!*

Tom's heart was still racing as he clambered out of the bush.

"Tom!"

Looking up, he saw Elenna rushing through the trees towards him, wide-eyed with anxiety. She had an arrow fitted to her bow.

"I'm all right!" he called, as she drew up, panting. He reached for his sword, then remembered Petorix had taken it. *It could be anywhere!*

Kaaaaaaark!

Tom and Elenna both froze at the cry from overhead. Then Tom spotted Petorix through the leaves. Her wings were tucked in as she hurtled down, fast as a spear. "Look out!" he yelled.

He shoved Elenna aside, just as the

Beast exploded through the branches above in a shower of twigs and leaves.

Tom ducked low, feeling the wind as Petorix swooped overhead, talons slicing. Her tail whipped out behind her. Blood pounding in his ears, and barely thinking, Tom threw himself at it, arms stretching out wide. He clung on to the tail with all his strength, and his stomach dropped as the Beast jerked him up into the air once again.

In a moment they were above the branches, surging higher. The Beast flicked her tail, like a horse trying to rid itself of a fly.

Not this time, Petorix... Tom clung on grimly. Using all the strength in his arms and legs, he began to haul himself higher, using the Beast's scales as hand and footholds.

The *Chronicles of Avantia* came back to him – the story of how Tanner had defeated Petorix. *If I could just get on to her back, like Tanner did...*

He heaved himself higher, until he could almost reach her shoulder blades. Petorix beat her wings furiously, swooping in circles. Tom pressed himself in closer to her cold, slippery body. In the *Chronicles*, he remembered, Tanner had a sword. *I haven't even got a butter knife!*

He cast a quick glance at the treetops below. But what he saw made his jaw drop.

Firepos was soaring low over the forest. And on her back was a man with long dark hair, holding on tight to the giant bird's feathers. A man Tom had seen on countless paintings and tapestries… *Tanner!*

Tom frowned. Even at this distance, he could tell that Tanner was weak, his face pale and his brow sweaty.

The hero looked up and caught his eye. Tom saw a deep determination in his gaze. Then Tanner drew his own sword, and raised it high…

Tom had hardly realised what was happening before Tanner hurled the weapon. The sword flew, flashing as it spun, end over end.

Digging his fingers in among the Beast's scales, Tom reached out with his free hand. *Got to…catch it…*

Then the worn leather of the hilt smacked into his palm, and he closed

his fingers tight around it.

Petorix swivelled her head, and
her horrible tongue came lashing
out, trying to reach him. Tom swung

himself aside, then swiped down hard at the Beast's neck.

THUNK!

He felt the blade pass through skin, flesh and bone, and the sword rang in his grip. For a moment, the Beast's head remained in place, before tumbling away through the sky. At the same time, the Beast's wings went limp and folded around her body. Then, like mist clearing, Petorix vanished completely.

Tom dropped like a stone, faster and faster... *This time there'll be no lucky branch to save me...*

He closed his eyes.

Thump!

His body jolted as he hit something unexpected. It felt soft and hard at the same time, like a tightly bundled bale of hay. Hands closed over his shoulders, holding him in place.

Tom opened his eyes. He was swooping through the air, sprawled across the feathered back of Firepos. It was Tanner who held him. Up close, Tom saw that the hero's face was paler than ever and slick with sweat.

They descended, rustling leaves as they passed through the canopy of the forest. Then – *whumph!* – Firepos landed in the clearing on outstretched talons and folded her wings. Elenna came running from the trees, together with Rufus, his red robes flapping.

Tanner smiled weakly at Tom. Then his eyes rolled back in his head. He toppled off Firepos's back and slumped into Rufus's arms.

He's dying, Tom realised, with a stab of horror. Quickly he slid to the ground himself. Digging inside his tunic, he brought out the fragment of eggshell. "Will this do?" he asked. "Can you heal him?"

Rufus frowned. "I'm not sure."

Tom's heart sank. *Tanner looks almost dead already,* he thought. *What if it's all been for nothing? What if I disappear here, in the past? What if Elenna never met me – will she disappear too?* His head began to hurt, and he clutched at it.

He looked down and gasped. Already he could see right through his own hands to the grass below. He peered at Elenna and saw that she was starting to fade too.

The magic of the stone circle is wearing off, he realised. *We're returning to our own time!*

There was a rushing in Tom's ears, and the world began to blur. It was happening faster and faster now… The earth shook, and thunder rolled. Tom could almost feel himself falling forward through time. And as he fell, one thought burned in his mind.

Ria's won. She's killed Tanner. Which means I was never born…

The last of the thunder died away, and Tom opened his eyes.

He stood on the grass, back in the middle of the stone circle. He turned

and saw Elenna beside him, looking
just as dazed as he felt.

"What happened?" she murmured.

As Tom was about to reply, he saw
Aduro just beyond the circle, staring
at them in astonishment. "You're
back!" said the old man. His eyes
looked moist. "I feared…well…I'm
just so glad to see you!"

Tom ran forward and hugged Aduro
tightly. He felt Elenna join in the hug,
and for a moment they clung to each
other in joyful silence.

"What happened?" asked Aduro at
last, as they broke apart. "Did you
travel back in time?"

Tom nodded, then frowned. "But we
might have failed. We got Tanner the
antidote, but he was dying, and…"

He tailed off, but Aduro smiled. "No, Tom," said Aduro. "You succeeded. You must have. If you hadn't, you wouldn't be standing here now."

Elenna looked at Tom. And slowly, they grinned at each other. *Aduro's right*, Tom realised. *Somehow, Tanner must have survived.*

"What about Ria?" said Elenna. "We lost her in the forest. Did she return to the stone circle?"

Aduro shook his head. "Perhaps she met her fate there, in the past."

Tom wasn't so sure. After facing Ria so many times, he knew she had a knack for wriggling out of danger. *She might still be out there somewhere. Waiting. And maybe, one day, I'll have to face her again...*

That evening, Tom and Elenna climbed down into the Gallery of Tombs at King Hugo's palace, followed by Daltec and Aduro. As they gathered around Tanner's sarcophagus, Tom's heart skipped a beat. Had they really saved the hero?

"*Here lies a hero*," read Aduro, running his forefinger across the letters carved in the stone. "*Laid to rest in his fifty-third year*."

"Phew!" breathed Elenna.

Tom felt warm relief flood through him. *We did it!*

Daltec blew dust from the cover of a hefty leather-bound tome and opened it. "Let's see what the *Chronicles of Avantia* have to say," he said, and cleared his throat. "*So Rufus crushed the shell of Petorix's egg, and mixed it into a potion of healing*," he read out loud. "*No sooner had the potion passed Tanner's lips, than the hero was revived. He lived to fight again, having stood before the very gates of Death.*"

Elenna punched Tom's arm. "Told you!" she said, grinning. "Everything's back to how it was."

"Not quite," said Daltec. He raised an eyebrow as he read more. "*Avantia owes much to a strange, handsome young warrior. A farm boy known as Tom, who helped Tanner to defeat the Beast…then vanished entirely.*"

"*Handsome*?" said Elenna, wrinkling her nose. "And what about his brilliant friend Elenna, who fights at his side on every Quest?"

Tom smiled. "Don't worry. I'm sure the *Chronicles* will tell a hundred tales of Tom *and* Elenna. The stories just haven't been written yet!"

CONGRATULATIONS, YOU HAVE COMPLETED THIS QUEST!

At the end of each chapter you were awarded a special gold coin. The QUEST in this book was worth an amazing 14 coins.

Look at the Beast Quest totem picture overleaf to see how far you've come in your journey to become

MASTER OF THE BEASTS.

The more books you read, the more coins you will collect!

Do you want your own
Beast Quest Totem?

1. Cut out and collect the coin below
2. Go to the Beast Quest website
3. Download and print out your totem
4. Add your coin to the totem

www.beastquest.co.uk

READ THE BOOKS, COLLECT THE COINS!
EARN COINS FOR EVERY CHAPTER YOU READ!

550+ COINS
MASTER OF THE BEASTS

410 COINS
HERO

350 COINS
WARRIOR

230 COINS
KNIGHT

180 COINS
SQUIRE

44 COINS
PAGE

8 COINS
APPRENTICE

550+
515
480
445
410
395
380
365
350
320
290
260
230
217
206
191
180
146
112
78
44
30
19
8